BARTER WORLD

PAM GLENN

CLASS
ACTION
INK

PORTLAND, OREGON, 2009

ISBN 978-0-9841530-0-8
LCCN 2009907828

Published by CLASS ACTION INK
Class Action Ink LLC
950 SW 21st Avenue, #511
Portland OR 97205

Order information is available at www.classactionink.com.

To Maung W. Myint and Christine J. Olson,
who made this book not only possible but necessary,
with great admiration, respect, and gratitude . . .
my first-born

TRADES & TRANSITS

A QUEEN'S RANSOM

ONCE UPON A TIME,
A YOUNG GIRL TRADED A STORY
FOR HER LIFE . . .

It has been said that she made her deal with the king before recorded history began, but in truth, the blue dome of the great mosque, tiled with prayers addressed to heaven, already lay in pieces where it had collapsed many years ago.

When her sister patted her cheek the second time, Scheherazade opened her eyes. In the small glow of an oil lamp in the far corner of the room she could see a dark boulder that was the servant woman seated on the floor by the wall, sleeping in her hooded robe. Scheherazade wondered if there was a message in the handful of stars framed by a small arched window near the ceiling.

"Tell me a story," her sister said quietly, as she had every night for nine hundred and eighty-six nights. And Scheherazade rose from the couch where she had rested after dinner with her sister and the servants. She slipped a long tunic over her striped silk sharovary. Holding her heavy black hair out of the way, she slid the rope of red beads over her head and settled them around her neck. On soft leather sandals, with her sister at her side, she walked to the end of the dark hall and knocked on the broad wooden door.

The manservant who opened it silently stepped aside to let the sisters enter. This room was as bright as the one they had left was dim. Shallow pottery lamps burned in niches in the walls and on a low table. Seated on his couch, King Schariar watched Scheherazade approach. She wore the red necklace he had given her every night she started a new story. So the long, long tale of Aladdin would end tonight and a new one begin.

"Listen, my royal master, and you shall hear . . . " she started, as she always had. From the first night, she had found the words that honored him as supreme ruler, her own lord, and a man longing to hear a story that would lead his imagination away from the cares of the world and the burdens of power.

"Come, be seated." He waved toward her accustomed place on the flowered rug by his couch. "We are eager to hear what you have brought us."

Samarkand had many beautiful mosques, and universities filled with scholars winkling wisdom from great texts. But the king, who prayed five times each day, and sometimes once again before he slept, and loved beauty and knowledge as much . . . *more* than any other man

. . . loved the great bazaar best of all. Royalty was in his blood, yes, but he breathed commerce.

News of caravans arriving from the east had always rendered him sleepless with anticipation. He postponed meetings with his advisors to slip out to the market, disguised, and watch people from the farthest reaches of his realm, and beyond, trade rice and goats for skins dyed in the stone vats of Africa and fragrant spices from unnamed islands in distant seas.

On just such a visit, he had given a golden bracelet that once belonged to his dead wife to a caravan merchant in exchange for two stone necklaces, one of twilight blue lapis, one of blood red carnelian. The man had served him tea and talked about his travels. The transaction was easily made, the bracelet being more valuable than the necklaces. But the merchant's tales of the thief and the camel; of the murderous twin brothers at the oasis; of the ruby as big as an egg, made up any difference. And the smooth, cool stones and exotic silk knots inspired the king to imagine lives he would never know.

When he returned to the palace, Schariar laid the stone necklaces in a niche in the wall of his sleeping chamber where he could see them as he discussed affairs of state with his counselors and generals. Sometimes he held the red necklace cupped in his hand and smoothed a bead with the pad of his thumb as he paced and pondered.

Schariar's first queen had been the older daughter of the king of Tashkent, ten days to the north and east of

Samarkand. Their fathers had arranged the marriage. Schariar saw his wife the first time at their elaborate wedding. She smiled at him during the feast and never again. She slept with him one night and made one son. Her agents pillaged the country for riches as relentlessly as an invading army, demanding tributes for the queen's treasuries; and she spent, constantly, lavishly, on entertainments and favored friends.

For eleven years, Schariar looked the other way. Then his father died, and Schariar found himself the newly anointed ruler of a country increasingly pressured by warring neighbors.

For five more years, Schariar let his neighbors, and his wife, do what their natures led them to do, while he learned to rule his lands wisely and well. He taught his son how to ride and fight; how to select a strong horse and a sound blade; how to distinguish wise counsel from advice that might lead him astray.

In the sixth year of Schariar's reign, marauders from the north crossed the border, attacking settlements and stealing herds and women. The king called his generals to Samarkand to plan ways for his army to repel the assaults. Together they spent their days discussing military strategies, their nights eating and telling stories of their old campaigns.

Leaving General Douban, his trusted friend from boyhood, in charge of the city, Schariar, with his son and three other generals, led a small army north to survey the border and quell disturbances. They visited sacked villages and encampments, taking reports from survivors.

After two months, Schariar and his son rode home, leaving troops under the generals' command to deal with any new violence. They crossed high plains, forded wild rivers, and slept under the high summer sky. They browned in the sun and the wind. The king was proud of his strong, swift son: He'd never seen a better rider. And on those rare occasions that required a fist or a blade, the boy was . . . sinew, tough as rope.

Two days out of Samarkand they encountered a northbound caravan and asked for news of home. In keeping with his visits to the bazaar, Schariar introduced himself and his son as army scouts returning from the frontier. They enjoyed the masquerade until, over dinner, gossip turned to palace rumors of the queen and the general.

The massacre of the daughters, as the people came to think of it, began the day after the beheading of General Douban.

Schariar had returned to the city without fanfare. He sent his son to bring him the grand vizier, his most trusted advisor, and entered the palace by a little-used door in the north wall. Upon finding the queen and the general alone together in the private audience room next to his sleeping chamber, he called for the captain of the palace guards.

Silently the queen handed him the gold bracelet he

had given her on the birth of their son. At Schariar's command, the guards strangled the queen and imprisoned the general, whose life had already abandoned his heart.

The following morning, pale from outrage and a sleepless night, King Schariar emerged from his chamber and ordered that one hundred daughters from good families be brought to the palace and housed in the suite of rooms formerly occupied by the queen's servants and attendants, who had returned to their villages.

For several weeks, graceful, dignified young women arrived at the palace from every corner of the realm. After they had settled in, Schariar selected a new bride from among them. The marriage and wedding feast were held that evening, and the newlyweds spent the night together in the king's chamber.

When he awoke, the king delivered his new wife to the captain of the guards and ordered her execution. He ate a light breakfast and met with his counselors to deal with matters of state.

In the afternoon, he visited the harem and selected a new bride. In order not to raise alarm among the others, he invited the young woman to dance for him and his guests. But later that evening she was brought into his presence dressed for the wedding that followed. As her predecessor had, Schariar's third bride shared a banquet and his bed and died by royal decree the next morning.

With King Schariar's fourth wedding, and the death of his fourth queen, the story of the daughters traveled on the winds, and the parents of Samarkand trembled to hear it.

Deeply disturbed by his usually temperate king's domestic reign of terror, Schariar's grand vizier walked to the palace in dread each morning and returned home more dispirited each evening. He no longer joined his friends for tea in the late afternoon, but lay on his bed with his dead wife's scarf covering his face.

On the day that the queens in the royal mausoleum outnumbered the young women in the royal harem, King Schariar's grand vizier took to his bed. He stopped eating and started to disappear. Hoping that sunlight might rekindle the fire in his heart, his servants carried him into the garden on the bench where he lay motionless, except for the slight movement where his shallow breathing stirred the white silk draped across his head and shoulders.

Scheherazade, the grand vizier's older daughter, approached him in the courtyard, where the pomegranate tree cast a shadow like iron flowers on her father's blue robe and sad, pale feet. She sat on the edge of the stone fountain, whose music had failed for the first time to bring him peace, and took his cool, dry hand in hers.

The servants watched from the darkened doorway as the young girl spoke to the body on the bench too quietly for them to hear her words. At one point they were startled to hear the grand vizier cry out; then his daughter continued to speak.

A short time later, he groaned aloud, pulled the scarf from his face and sat up, wincing with the effort. Scheherazade took the silk from his hands, wet it in the fountain, and gently wiped his brow.

The next morning the grand vizier went to the palace to recommend his daughter for marriage to the king. Astounded by the request, Schariar refused. With his remaining strength, Scheherazade's father pressed her petition until the king relented.

"Bring her to me, then, day after tomorrow." He frowned as his grand vizier left the audience hall. The man seemed old, suddenly, and slow.

At the appointed time, Scheherazade accompanied her father into the king's presence with her younger sister at her side. Schariar was impressed by her quiet grace.

"I haven't seen you since you were a child." He smiled to set her at ease. "And who is this?"

Scheherazade set her hand on her sister's shoulder. "This is my younger sister, Dinarzade, your majesty. I brought her with me because we have never been apart. May she come with me? To wake with me and bid me farewell in the morning?"

"Ah. Of course. She is welcome, as long as she understands the nature of our arrangement."

When Dinarzade, who was staring at her toes, nodded, Schariar's servants placed a small bench for her at the foot of his bed. That evening, after the wedding and the feast, when the guests had departed and the king motioned Scheherazade into his chamber, Dinarzade followed, and soon fell asleep at their feet.

Lying on his side on his couch, Schariar spoke quietly with his new bride. Looking at her soft profile in the candlelight, it struck him for the first time how young she was. He rose from his bed and walked to the niche in the wall where the strings of red and blue beads lay jumbled together. Pulling them apart, he slid the lapis necklace over his head and set it around his neck. Holding the red beads in his hands, he offered them to Scheherazade: "I'd like you to have these. My wedding gift to you."

Taking them in her cupped palms, Scheherazade gazed at thirty-seven perfect stones the color of life itself and her heart beat a quiet message of hope.

When the first bird sang, an hour before dawn, Dinarzade awoke and patted her sleeping sister's face. "Tell me a story, oh my sister," she said, just as they had planned, and Scheherazade turned to the king and asked, "May I grant her wish, your majesty?"

"It can do no harm," Schariar replied.

So Scheherazade tucked her sister back under the blanket on the small bed at the foot of the king's bed and seated herself on a blue rug beside his couch. Then, holding the beads resting closest to her heart, she began, as she would for the thousand nights that followed, "Listen, my royal master, and you shall hear . . ."

By the time the merchant in her story met the genie at the well, the sun was rising over the palace, and Dinarzade had fallen sound asleep.

9

"I shall have to stop now, your majesty, and finish the story when my sister is awake to hear it."

King Schariar himself wanted to know how the merchant's predicament resolved itself. "You will finish telling this tale tonight so that she is not disappointed."

The servants looked at each other but did not let their eyes show any curiosity at this new development.

The first year Scheherazade told him the old stories from the old times, when her own father's fathers had herded horses on the high plains, and Schariar's father's fathers were gods. She always stopped when there was more to say, and began at that very point the next night.

Sometimes she rose and left the room at a moment of such suspense that the servants coughed and stretched their arms and legs to release the tension. And the king, dismayed by the interruption, allowed their antics to give him vicarious relief while he maintained a posture of regal calm.

"Is that the end of the story, then?" he asked her one evening when he let irritation get the better of him.

"Oh, no, your majesty," Scheherazade replied as she traced the border of the rug on which she sat with one slender finger. "But that is all the time we have tonight. Your majesty needs rest to stay healthy and vigorous as you subdue our enemies and conduct the affairs of the realm. Your vizier has told me this is true."

My vizier, your esteemed father. Schariar relied on his beard to mask his smile at her quiet audacity.

"You are right, of course. Certainly, the king's good health is in the interests of all. Shall we consider your brevity to be a royal gift to the people? Not a typical gift, but a wise one in many ways." As the sigh slipped out of his mouth like the genie released from the lamp, his young wife raised her eyes to his and smiled.

Schariar's servants listened in rapt silence to the adventures of Sinbad. They chuckled with polite restraint at the tales of Haroun al Rashid and his women. But the king sensed that Scheherazade's own favorite stories were about moments of magical transformation, and he was moved by her affection to love them best too. It eased a royal headache to have the problems of the world reduced to a clever negotiation between a camel driver and a fairy disguised as a dog.

Sitting on a carpet that would never carry her farther than the dawn, Scheherazade spun out the old tales of love and magic and deceit. No matter how hard she might rub the lamp that cast a warm light over the king reclining against his silken cushions, that clay jar would never produce the smallest genie with the least wish-granting powers. Still, for one thousand mornings Scheherazade awoke with a new story to tell her husband. And finally, the king, whose heart had learned to trust again, released her from her task to live at his side in peace.

That same afternoon, Scheherazade threw the lamp that had witnessed her ordeal onto the courtyard tiles and buried the sharp pieces under a lemon tree in the palace garden. She bundled the rug and bound it firmly with a heavy cord.

Dressed as a servant in black, with a manservant at her side and the rug balanced on her head, she walked to the market in the center of the city. The man led her to a merchant from the caravan recently arrived from the east, whom he approached with the time-honored greeting. The merchant offered him tea. They sipped and chatted about the places and the weather the merchant had seen in his travels. The queen sat on her bundle and glanced at the other sellers' wares displayed on the ground nearby.

After a while, the servant said, "I think we have something that may interest you."

"I already have very many rugs, as you see," the merchant replied.

"Yes," said the servant. "But they are not like this rug." As Scheherazade stood and moved aside, the merchant untied the cord and opened the rug upon the ground.

"It is a good rug. I can see that. It is well made, a traditional pattern. Small, solid knots. Lovely colors." The merchant nodded gravely at Scheherazade, as though she might have woven it herself. "But I still have a very long way to go: I'm selling rugs now, not adding to my stock."

"This is not just any rug, my friend," the servant insisted in a low voice, so that none nearby could overhear. "This is the rug on which our Queen Scheherazade told her stories to the king. More stories than there are flowers in this excellent rug. More stories than there are stars in the night sky. Just imagine!"

Scheherazade's fame as a storyteller had traveled the caravan routes. In exchange for her rug, the merchant gave the servant bolts of his best blue, red and purple silk, a jade horse, five brass bells, and a tall porcelain jar filled with long leaf black tea. As they talked, Scheherazade turned her back to them and folded and retied the rug, with the red stone necklace wrapped inside.

"And this is for you, miss." The merchant rested his cupped hands in hers. "For your patience."

She looked carefully at his face: It was not like any face she had seen before, and she knew she would never see it again. She nodded and then followed the servant back through the marketplace, holding the small object concealed against her waist, where it rattled quietly as she walked.

The servant delivered the queen and her purchases to the royal suite by a little-used palace door and returned to his work. Scheherazade set the merchant's gift on the stone window sill: A filigree ivory ball, slightly larger than her fist, with a smaller one just like it inside, and a smaller one inside that one, and so on . . . and so on. She counted five altogether, covered in carved flowers. There may have been more.

Later that afternoon Scheherazade, dressed in a queen's lavender robe and a necklace of silver pomegranates, entered the apartments of the harem. One by one she helped thirty-seven young women pack their possessions and return to their families. There was much rejoicing, in the palace and in all of Samarkand.

At twilight, Scheherazade found Dinarzade walking with their father among the lemon trees in the palace garden. "And what can I give you, my steadfast, beloved sister?" she asked, taking both of her small hands into her own.

Reaching up to touch her sister's cheek, Dinarzade smiled softly: "Listen, your majesty, and you shall hear how long, long ago a young girl traded the world of her imagination for the heart of a powerful king."

CARAVAN

In the weeks that followed, the merchant had a good trip, all the way to Baghdad and north toward the Bosporus. The days grew cooler and shorter, and his route was mercifully free of thieves and wild animals. In Aleppo he traded his remaining bolts of silk for five more rugs.

By the time he reached Constantinople it was already too late to return home before winter closed not just the high mountain passes but long sections of the caravan road itself.

Nine years before, he'd tried to outrace the bitter winds and been trapped by heavy snow in a small village just a few days from his own. He spent a very long winter with a herder's family who didn't have enough food for themselves, even, and were too decent to refuse him shelter. He still remembered the bone-chilling cold; the small, smoky fire; the hunger. He and his hosts wore every piece of clothing and wrapped themselves in every threadbare rug and skin they owned; they hibernated like beasts, sleeping—or pretending to sleep—to ignore the gnawing in their stomachs. Rather than take that chance again, he would spend this winter in a city, with food and strangers with stories at each glowing hearth.

He entered the city at the full moon and drank tea with his friends in the market, who gave him news of recent goods and prices. There were two ships in port, with merchants buying for return trips, one to Venice, one all the way to Antwerp.

The next day he followed one of the men from the market to the quay where the Italian ship was tied up, a crew already loading freight into her hold. Brokers and clerks recorded the cargo and gave each seller a piece of paper in exchange for his goods.

His friend from the market tried to explain how such a paper could be exchanged for gold at the Italian traders' bank, but the caravan merchant didn't believe that any piece of paper was as good as gold, or that any clutch of gold coins was equal to a rug or a bundle of hides. He wanted to see what he was getting, to hold it and assess its worth. Only a fool would take a sheet of paper for a palmful of pearls. And he'd heard about the bankers: Among themselves they traded one piece of paper for another. Could anything be crazier!

The merchant returned to his waiting camel and walked beside her along the wharf to where the ship from Antwerp was tied up. With his friend acting as interpreter, he and a German merchant arrived at an agreement. In exchange for twenty-seven copper jars filled with spices and one filled with opals, all sealed with thick red wax, the camel merchant gave the German his entire stock, including the small blue rug where Scheherazade once told stories to thaw the heart of a king. Tied inside, forgotten in the dark, lay a necklace of stones as red as blood.

HOLBEIN'S BLOODSTONES

SEVERAL CENTURIES AGO, THE BEST
PAINTER IN ALL THE KINGDOM
TRADED HIS ART FOR STONES . . .
AND STONES FOR ART.

Lady Mary Guildford sat for one of my first London portraits in her best fur cloak and russet silk gown garlanded with gold chains; her most elaborate gable hood; four rings and the pendant with gems and pearls that Lord Henry gave her on their wedding. The sprig of rosemary was my own idea, a small tribute to the connection between man and wife. Rosemary, to encourage memory. And because I hoped to watch her tuck it into her bodice, against a breast as white and soft as my Elsbeth's.

The first letter from home said they were all well, my wife and her boy Franz, along with our Philip, and infant Catherine, born after my departure from Basel the previous September. That the tannery Elsbeth had inherited from her first husband continued to prosper under her management came as no surprise: I had married her as much for her ability to run a business alongside a household, as for her generous temperament and warm bed.

In those early days in London I longed for the hours when weariness and darkness used to fling us together at night like sacks on a shelf, to restore ourselves in sleep, sex and laughter.

That is what I have missed most here: laughter. These English take life very seriously. Even the Mores' harmonious household had its rivalries and jealousies. I noticed early that Sir Thomas More's jests were often made at someone else's expense. Oh, he was generous with commissions and introductions to members of his circle, which overlapped with shifting centers of power at court that rippled out from King Henry all the way to the Netherlands and France, but there was something mean in him.

The King's courtiers prize the wit of word games that rarely cross the borders of language. The same impulse that leads them to wear many layers of silks and velvets, folded and fastened in complicated tucks and pleats, directs their imaginations to verbal puzzles that leave me sitting dumbfounded among chuckling, sherry-sipping aristocrats, wishing for a tankard of beer and a song.

I recall the time, shortly before I came here, young Franz asked about a sound at our dinner table, the squeak of a fart suppressed by being sat upon. Straight-faced, his mother informed him that a mouse had sneezed. There is none of that fanciful silliness in this world of court politics and favor-trading.

With my Dutch patron Erasmus's letter of introduction, I had been warmly received by More. The days of my visit lengthened into honorary residence in his home. By the time I received a royal commission to decorate the pavilion being built for the celebration of England's new treaty with France, I was well aware, from dinner-table conversation, of tensions developing in the royal household.

"He has rusticated her." More put down his spoon. "In truth, himself."

Lady Alice raised her eyebrows.

"Absented himself from her bed."

"Dearest!"

"I know." He glanced at the children, whose attention was suddenly focused on their food—their way of leaving the room without interrupting the adults to ask permission, and the rude noise of scraping chairs.

"This cannot be a good thing. In his desire for a son he has come to see Queen Catherine's inability to give him one as stubbornness."

It struck me as strange that news of the royal bedchamber should be a matter for conversation, even in the house of such a trusted advisor to the King. And what was to be drawn from this rumor, and all the other tidbits of gossip constantly in the air like chaff in the winds of royal favor?

Sir Thomas passed a silver platter to his right with instructions to his daughter in Latin or Italian. Or Portuguese, for all I knew.

"Yes, Father," Margaret replied, and then, "Mr. Holbein, may I offer you more meat?" in perfect German. More's daughters studied languages and sciences with tutors as advanced in their fields as Nicholas Kratzer, the King's astronomer. Their father challenged them at table with questions in strange languages about subjects I myself had debated among men in taverns. But I had never before met women with knowledge of such matters or any interest in discussing them. I myself far prefer the quiet hours of ink, charcoal and paint, something tangible to show for my days.

That first December I met Kratzer at More's table. The royal astronomer was charming and extremely well versed in sciences, and I admired his gracious nature almost as much as his genius. The King's pavilion for the treaty celebration gave us our first opportunity to work together.

Kratzer's extraordinary learning and powers of thought seemed to be discounted by some as magic, perhaps because he concerned himself with matters far beyond most men's comprehension. While I, with my gold-tipped brush, have a talent for capturing what they already see in the glass and want preserved, a parlor trick alongside his intimate familiarity with the elements of heaven and earth.

That evening the astronomer wore a rope of red beads, as much to stimulate conversation as for decorative effect. In response to Miss Margaret's question, he told us that he discovered the beads wrapped in a small rug he had recently bought from one of the German merchants in the Steelyard. Kratzer knew the man's merchandise was of the highest quality, so quick inspection of a corner of the piece convinced him that it was well made and handsome.

Upon opening the bundle in his rooms, Kratzer discovered the red stone necklace. When he tried to return it, the merchant refused to receive it, or take payment for it, on the principle that since he had been unaware of its existence, he could not be said to have owned it and therefore could not sell it, or keep it, once it had found its way into someone else's hands.

This tale generated a lively discussion about ownership and possession that lasted the rest of the meal, during which I determined to have the red necklace. I sensed that it had powers I would only perceive or enjoy once it was mine.

As controller of the royal household, Sir Henry Guildford was in charge of the May fête. He oversaw construction and decoration of the hall, along with arranging and scheduling all the day's events, and the feeding of several hundred noble guests. I had met him too at More's table, but he was a different man at his work, orchestrating the King's elaborate affair within the constraints of calendar and purse.

I was one artist among many. And while I had been commissioned to paint the triumphal arch for the banquet hall and theater ceiling, I also picked up other small jobs that no one else had been hired for.

Kratzer looked at my drawing for the theater ceiling—*terra firma* surrounded by the world sea—and suggested the overlay we made to show all seven planets, each in its heavenly house, the whole zodiac anchored by the two poles. A much more imposing conception than my initial scheme, and very much to Sir Henry Guildford's liking.

The king came in April to review our progress and declared himself well pleased with all finished work. He made suggestions to Guildford and approved my plan to paint the zodiac and planets on gauze to be laid over the rest, so that the entire earth and sea might be visible through it.

Over supper that evening I thanked Kratzer for improving the project, and the King's opinion of it.

"I admire your work, my friend. It was a pleasure to help, in whatever small way."

In that spirit we arranged a trade, he having even less gold than I: In exchange for the red necklace I offered to paint his portrait.

The next week, we put the finishing touches on the banquet hall and theater. In the evenings, I painted a miniature of Kratzer, as a study for the portrait, which pleased him so that he gave me the necklace. I didn't complete the final painting until later in the year, when the magic of the necklace had already done its work.

The treaty celebration day dawned clear and warm. With all participants dressed in beautiful bright silks, the tournaments, pageants, and musical performances of all sorts proceeded according to plan.

The ball that night was the most elegant anyone could recall, the banquet unparalleled for excellence and variety of foods and flowers, tributes and toasts continuing until dawn. King Francis was loud in his enjoyment and King Henry even more generous, therefore, with his praise and his purse.

What is the appeal of a roasted peacock? The bird's primary energy goes to self-decoration and display; surely there is no tenderness left to the meat. And still the fowl is borne to the high table on a silver tray, surrounded by his own plumage, to the sighs and applause of his human counterparts, who draw no lesson from such a bitter end to a life of vanity.

With the festival day behind us, Guildford asked me to paint his portrait, and one of his wife, and I was glad to do it, knowing that he was a good man to work for, and prompt to pay without argument.

On my first visit to his home, I laid down enough charcoal and ink to clarify my sense of Sir Henry's face, sketches for the final drawing that became the basis for the formal portrait. I also met Lady Guildford, who seemed less eager to have her likeness drawn than to please her husband.

"Those beads are dull," I said. Not thinking that they might be more than beads—a rosary, the treasured gift of her dead husband. Before Guildford. I made serious errors at that first meeting: I thought her indifferent where she was polite; superficial where she was kind; vain where she was mindful of my comfort. Sir Henry fostered this confusion by treating her almost as a child, which she was not, but a woman in her own right and equally skilled at directing a household or a conversation with the appearance of effortlessness.

She had a modesty so rare that anyone might overlook it from ignorance. That being the significant attribute of humility, that it does not put itself forward. Lady Mary was exceptional in this self-promoting society by the very fact that she did not stand out. Perhaps could not, even if her life depended on it.

As I came to know her, drawing her, I was smitten . . . with reverence. If she wanted the wooden beads, I would not argue, but I brought the bloodstone necklace to our next sitting. They glowed against the dark fabric of her gown. And she understood that there is no point in putting something you cannot see into a picture. If the rosary can be said to represent Christ's passion and death—and even her husband's in battle at Marignan—then what better color than the red of blood? Also for love.

I have fewer illusions than many men: I do not fool myself, as some do who are trying every moment to mollify God with manners. I please God as I can with the talent He gave me to limn the likenesses of His creatures and the stories of His works as they are told us in the Bible.

My behavior will never redeem me in God's eyes. I eat too much and drink too much, run to the promise of money and fame as fast as the next man. So distant from my wife, I long for the company only a woman can provide . . . and a certain kind of woman at that. Sophisticated London ladies are easily seduced by paintings and amusing conversation and have no sweetness in them. They flutter. It is hard to imagine that Lady Lambeth or the Misses Charteret could sit still for the crudest sketch.

Lady Mary was patient with slow growth and change. Also observant. Her comments were always worth the listening; strung together, like her rosary, they slowly revealed events that were obscure to me then. I felt tensions whose origins were like the charcoal lines under layers of bright pigments that hardened and crazed in the tempestuous winds of the court.

I had seen her needlework, surely the finest anywhere. A small tapestry on the dining room wall was a solid tissue of individual silk stitches as fine as only my finest brush or point might make: thread of gold, and every other color of flowers, berries and leaves, and hidden among them a fanciful bird, green and red and blue, its round eye peeking straight out at me. A jest. I felt someone watching me eat and saw the bird's eye trained on me and laughed aloud. After dinner, when the others had left, I walked around the table and found that the eye stared equally at any person anywhere in the room.

Where, I asked her, did you see that creature? But she had not, only heard an account of such a bird that had the power of human speech, she said, many years ago. Her mind had created and held its own picture of the thing until time came to release it into her own world the best way she knew how. Her smile anticipated laughter, but I didn't laugh; I understood completely. She did in thread what I do with paint.

When it came to her sitting, I recommended that we include her inlaid wooden box full of bright yarns, tinsell and floss; perhaps a corner of the frame with work in progress. But she preferred to hold her book and rosary.

She knew the reformed church was replacing her traditional religion, and a handful of men rewriting the laws of the realm to suit their monarch's purposes. The portrait was her way of recording the position from which she would not change, whatever the King's temper and the fashions that followed it. I didn't know enough then to fear for her.

First I drew her in ink with her dun beads. For the painting, she substituted the red string, to please me, I thought, and, I realized later, to draw attention to them. In this way she called us to perceive her own direct connection to God: She could read the book. She could say the prayers. No priest needed to be paid to grant her access to heaven; or, unpaid, had the power to obstruct it. And the beads, the book, refreshed her love of God and man; she had no need of the new reforms.

When I drew the study, her face was slightly turned, her eyes directed toward the wall nearby where Sir Henry's portrait already hung. Her lips curved in a slight smile. Had my painting followed that sketch, her gaze would have connected them as strongly as one felt they were connected in life.

Six weeks later, Lady Mary sat for her portrait. She faced me directly, eyes straight ahead, unsmiling, watching me as I worked. She appeared calm: That shows in the finished work. But the lightness of spirit and sweet affection in the sketch had gone. Similarly, her manner with Lord Henry was gracious, kind—solicitous for his health and needs—but lacked the light touch that had caught a fancy bird in a web of bright thread.

Lord Henry seemed even busier with matters at court—and less inclined to report them in my presence— and more concerned with her wellbeing. "Are you feeling well, my dear?" and the like, even more than before.

We never know another man's marriage. And Henry Guildford had two, one to Lady Mary; and another, vastly more complicated, to the King, whose daily life only ran as smoothly as it did by Guildford's constant work and attention to every detail. It is no exaggeration to say that despite the startling parade of women through the King's bed and affections, Guildford was the best wife Henry Tudor ever had. For all the good it did either of them in the end.

Imagine a palace with sixty rooms in active service. A kitchen to stock. Fires to lay and keep burning in each sleeping chamber and any hall where guests might meet or dine. Gardens producing fruits and vegetables all the year. Stables of beasts for hunting, drayage and meat. Flocks of fowl. Ponds stocked with fish for sport and food. The royal wardrobes and dressing tables, beds and basins. A constant tide of noble visitors through the place, with their needs known and anticipated before their arrival, to be housed as long as it suited them to stay. And whatever else in the way of extraordinary events, celebrations, the King's own travels to visit other heads of state. Furnishing Anne Boleyn's rooms, down the hall from the King's, when she first moved into the palace. Those were some of Sir Henry's domestic duties, directing all the work of staffs of servants and retainers.

While Henry Guildford understood the King's desire for a legitimate male heir, he had great respect for Queen Catherine. A humane man, he was no doubt appalled by the King's treatment of his wife of many years, and knew that if any blame can be said to attach to the failure to make a son, it must be shared equally by man and wife.

Lord Henry may have had the only ear at court where gossip stopped like a stone dropped down a well. He was reputed to have heard everything imaginable and never to have divulged a word of it, not even to the King, who knew better in that case than to insist.

Did Lord Henry share any of the hearsay with Lady Mary, or his opinions about what he knew to be true? Did he describe, to anyone, Anne Boleyn's accusations that led him to resign his post, despite the King's protest? I never knew.

Mary Guildford was as close with information as her husband, and therefore, in yet another way, his perfect mate. Herself the silken bird of her embroidered fancy, the partially concealed, bright-eyed observer, capable of speech but silent. Married to the royal helpmeet, and protecting him, and herself, the best way she knew how within the terms of her own temperament.

By the time I began the color portrait, she saw the clouds massing on the horizon, far beyond the blue sky I put at her back, and the fig tendrils reaching to grasp the curtain rod for support.

I never felt so . . . *safe* here as I did in the hours I spent in Lady Mary's company. Her actions and conversation were better lessons in godly life than you will find in books, by Erasmus or More or anyone else, who would bridle at the suggestion that a woman might be holy.

I carry her picture with me always. A miniature in a flat case; the lid folds back on its hinge to lap over the edge of whatever aristocrat's portrait I'm working on. From the upper right-hand corner, the slight smile and warm gaze she once directed at Lord Henry have shifted to me. She guides my work and guards my days.

If my years at court have taught me anything it is this: Everything changes, fame and favor along with the rest. The seeds of death are in all life, for man and woman, peacock and parrot, rumor and treaty. For God's own son, as we have been taught. And as King Henry knows better than most of us, a king—for all his wealth and power—is finally only a man.

I follow the new teachings as well as I know how, but find no joy or comfort in Luther's bare white church. And every morning I take the beads she gave me out of the drawer, touch the worn wood, and say the words that opened her daily conversation with God: *Hail, Mary, full of grace.*

MARY GUILDFORD'S
DAUGHTERS

When she was dying, Mary Guildford called her older daughter, Cecilia, to her bedside to give her her blessing. Since King Henry's suppression of the Church had made it dangerous for English Catholics to practice their religion openly, Lady Mary placed the string of red beads around Cecilia's neck and hoped silently that they would bring the girl the gift of peaceful purpose they'd brought her as a rosary.

Cecilia wore the necklace to church every Sunday to feel her mother's comforting presence in their cool weight.

In 1569, Cecilia gave the necklace to her first daughter, Mary, who, in turn, gave it to her first daughter, Cecilia, who eventually left it to her first daughter Mary. And so Scheherazade's red beads passed down through ten generations of first daughters, each named Cecilia or Mary after her maternal grandmother.

In the summer of 1742, the Mary of that generation boarded a ship bound for England's colony at Massachusetts Bay. Mary's husband John Willing, the youngest of several brothers, dreamed of farming his own land in the New World. In their trunk, in the pocket of Mary's winter coat, the red necklace crossed the sea, wrapped in a linen scarf.

In 1745, Mary Willing died giving birth to a daughter whose grief-stricken father named her Sarah. Mary's black wool coat lay in the trunk in their small house at the edge of Boston, and sometimes John would fish out the string of beads and hand them to the baby to play with, since there were no toys in the place. Sarah would clutch one of the red stones and knock it against the floorboards, or put it into her mouth to suck the faint sweetness of her mother's skin.

When she grew older, Sarah found the long-forgotten necklace in the trunk and slipped it over her head to feel the weight of the cool beads resting on her chest. She gazed at her reflection in the small mirror by the door and wondered how much she looked like the mother she had never seen.

BOUNTY

A VERY LONG TIME AGO, IN A RIVER VALLEY
WITH THE RICHEST EARTH THIS SIDE OF EDEN,
A FARMER TRADED HIS MENDING FOR THE
LOVE OF A BEAUTIFUL WOMAN.

"Breakfast, ladies!" Matthew threw handfuls of corn into the fenced yard and waited for the chickens to run from the henhouse *buck-bucking*. They pecked at the kernels and sidled into each other, wings flapping.

With his basket over his arm, the farmer stooped and entered the lean-to next to the barn, shooing the rooster aside. In the corner, big red Hilda nested on five eggs to keep them warm until they hatched. She clucked a warning as he collected eight eggs from the small piles of loose straw on the shelf where the other hens had laid them.

After he'd eaten his own breakfast of bread, butter and tea, Matthew closed the iron stove to smother the fire and put on his brown jacket. He returned to the barn and checked the cart wheels for soundness, then brought the tack from its wall peg into the stall to harness Lady for their trip to town.

He led the big gray into the yard and put the straw-filled basket of eggs on a folded blanket next to the driver's seat to cushion it. Then he went to the workbench in the barn, where he stored lumber and tools. One at a time he carried two wooden chests to the wagon, covered them with blankets, and fastened them in place with ropes.

The larger chest had four drawers and a small box built into the top for collars, studs and stays. Mr. Moon, the magistrate, had seen such a dresser in his travels and wanted one for his own use.

The smaller box had two shallow drawers with many dividers. Daniel Shoemaker lived in a cabin with his wife and four small children. He had ordered a chest to keep his needles, knives and other sharp blades and points out of the hands of his curious, agile brood.

Matthew climbed onto the wagon seat and slapped the horse's wide back lightly with the reins. Since the dirt road into town was badly rutted by weather and cart traffic, the jolting four-mile trip took almost two hours.

"It's just what I had hoped for, Mr. Wright." Moon slid each drawer open and shut several times, examining the dovetail corners and iron pulls. "So smooth!" He smiled appreciatively and reached toward the collar box on top of the chest. "May I?" Matthew stood back as the magistrate peered into the box.

"I've drawn up two copies of the bill," said Mr. Moon. "'In exchange for one cherry wood chest . . .' and so on,

'I grant Matthew Wright of this township permission to log my acre of land . . .' at thus-and-such a place, 'for three years, or until he shall have collected twenty cords of lumber and firewood . . .' and so forth."

He laid the sheets side by side on the hall table so they could both sign their names. At the bottom of each copy Mr. Moon wrote, *Received from Matthew Wright this date one cherry wood chest of drawers according to my requirements,* and initialed and dated them a second time. He folded one and handed it to Matthew, who tucked it into his coat pocket.

Matthew drove down the hill from Mr. Moon's house and across the bridge at the edge of town to Daniel Shoemaker's. The tall trees of the creek-side grove that shaded the roof to cool the cabin in summer made it cold and damp in winter. Daniel's joints ached every morning from October until April or even May. And since he worked with his hands, he kept a small fire in the grate on all but the warmest days. When it wasn't raining, his older children scoured the creek banks and roadsides for fallen twigs and branches.

Matthew knocked at the front door loudly enough to be heard over the tapping of the hammer, then entered the room where the cobbler worked at his bench while two children played in the corner near the baby's cradle.

"Matthew, you're a welcome sight! Come in."

"I won't keep you long, Daniel. But I've brought you something. Let me get it from the wagon."

Matthew carried the cabinet to the workroom and set it on the end of the bench.

"It's beautiful." Daniel opened and closed the drawers, remarking on the smallest details. "And a godsend. The children are too curious for safety. Maybe this will prevent the accident I fear." He nodded at a deep shelf above the front window. "If I put all the tools away each evening and put the box up there with the drawer pulls facing the wall, . . . well, that's about the best we can do. Thank you."

"Always glad to help." Matthew leaned against the workbench and ran his hand over a smooth, tanned skin. "Beautiful leather."

"Pair of boots for John Farmer. And you, what shall I make you for this box then? I have three of those skins, if you'd like shoes or boots from that same leather."

Matthew bent down to pull off one darkened boot and handed it to Daniel. "These are four years old now. You'll want to start breaking in a new pair so that they can go to work when these get too old to leave home."

The soles of Matthew's boots had been cut to the same last. By wearing each one on the left foot as often as the right, he had worn down the edges of the heels and soles evenly. He oiled the boots regularly, so that, while there were creases across insteps and toes, and the uppers bunched around his ankles, the leather would last another year or two.

"This is John Farmer's. Will it suit you?" Daniel held up one boot-in-progress.

"Looks just fine. Maybe a bit wider at the top." He examined the sole. "And a lower heel."

"In a month, or six weeks?"

"That would be good. And Daniel, one other thing: Mr. Moon has given me logging rights on his wood lot south of town. I'd be glad to bring you two cords."

Hands on his hips, Daniel grinned at his friend. "That would be a blessing indeed. We barely squeaked through last winter. What could I do to repay you?"

"Maybe some shoes for my boy Tom's children? Ann, Ruth and William. Would that be fair?"

"And a pair for Tom," Daniel added.

"Are you sure?"

"Little shoes don't take much leather, or time. Have Tom bring them by for me to measure, and I'll get started when I finish your boots."

"Make the children's shoes first, then Tom's and mine. They can go barefoot in this warm weather, but I want them shod by the time the leaves fall."

When Matthew drove the wagon into the mill yard, the wheel was silent, the grinding stone still. Sam came out to greet him and pass along village news. The blacksmith had been ill for weeks and was still coughing. The teacher was engaged to a man she'd grown up with in Boston and would return home to marry him at Christmas. And Jack Carpenter had died, leaving Sarah to raise and provide for their two sons and infant daughter.

"How ever will she get along?" Sam clapped his hands

against his heavy tan apron and a small cloud of flour rose into the air between them. "He was injured in that accident last March and never worked again. I think they used up their stores just nursing him until he passed away. They look so thin, Sarah and the children."

"I heard he'd fallen repairing Mr. Moon's barn roof." Matthew hefted a sack off the wagon bed and handed it to Sam, then lifted another just like it to his own shoulder and followed the miller through the doorway into the cool, dark interior. "Broke his back, did he?"

"Just set it down here." Sam pulled a book off the shelf and leafed through until he found Matthew's page. "Depends who's talking whether it was his back or some ribs. But everyone agrees it was the broken leg that killed him. Wound never healed. Fever took him in the end. So, we've got two sacks here. Forty pounds all told."

"You keep your four and put twenty on Sarah Carpenter's account and the balance on mine."

Sam made notes on three separate pages. "And will you be taking some with you this time?"

"I'll take five pounds to her now, and five more home with me."

Sam measured out two bags of fine milled flour and entered the amounts on each page. "That leaves her fifteen pounds on account . . . and you eleven. I was just making tea. Will you stay a while?"

They walked out into the sunlit yard together and Matthew put the flour sacks on the wagon bed next to the basket of eggs and another basket with a cloth over the top. He lifted the cloth and reached inside. "I'd better get on my way. Other errands still to do, and chores. But next time I'll stay longer. In the meantime, try these apples and let me know what you think." He handed Sam two large green apples streaked with bright pink.

"They smell fine! Thank you. And please give Sarah my regards."

"I'll do that." Matthew climbed onto the wagon seat and slapped the reins lightly along the horse's flank. "Hup, Lady, move along now."

The Carpenter boys ran from the field beside the creek when Matthew drew up near the house and climbed down from the wagon.

"Good morning. Is your mother at home?"

"She's inside, Mr. Wright," said Gideon, the older boy. "Bathing the baby."

"And how are you today?"

"Fine, thank you, Sir," they said in unison. But they were slow to smile and quieter than his own son had been at that age.

"Well, here's something for each of you." He pulled two apples from the basket and gave them to the boys, who took great white bites.

"Hello, Mr. Wright." Sarah Carpenter stood in the doorway, holding the baby against her shoulder. The indigo of her linen dress had leached to gray, and her cornflower blue eyes paled to match. Her skin was nearly as white as the baby's bonnet. As she crossed the yard toward him the sunlight gilded tendrils of fine blond hair that had escaped around the edges of her own cap. "What brings you here today?"

"I have some apples, and eggs fresh this morning." He followed her into the house and set the baskets on the table. "And there's a sack of flour in the wagon."

While he was outside, Sarah lifted a stoneware jug off a shelf near the stove and poured some of its contents into a small jar that she stoppered with a wooden plug.

"Here you are." Matthew set the flour on the table. "I thought that you might like to bake a pie."

"How very thoughtful. Thank you." Sarah held out the jar. "The boys and I tapped a few sugar maples last winter. This will sweeten your spoonbread."

"Will there be enough left for you and the children?"

"Oh, yes. Jack taught us well. We never run short of maple syrup and sugar."

"Can I put that back for you?" He set the jug on the shelf she pointed to. Not more than a couple of inches left—if that—he could tell by weight.

"Cozy room," he said, glancing briefly at the nearly empty shelves; limp garments hung on wall pegs; embers glowing in the grate; a patched kettle listing on the cooling stove. The baby, pink from her recent bath, cooed happily by her mother's ear.

What Matthew didn't see, in the pocket of the worn wool coat hanging on the back of the cabin door, was the string of carnelian beads, wrapped in the linen scarf in which they'd crossed the ocean on a ship filled with dream-seekers.

"I've left grain on your account at Sam's. Fifteen pounds, in addition to that," he nodded toward the table. "If you start to run low before I come back to town, send one of the boys to let me know."

"This is such a help. How can I possibly thank you?" Sarah jostled the baby, who burped loudly against her shoulder, and Matthew smiled to see her face soften in amusement.

"You gave me your maple syrup. I'm a wealthy man!" Turning away, he missed her fleeting frown.

Two weeks later, Matthew drove his wagon back into town with firewood from Mr. Moon's lot. At Shoemaker's, he and Daniel unloaded enough to stack rows six feet high the length of the south wall under the roof overhang.

"How is Sarah Carpenter?" Matthew asked as he jostled the last logs to a snug fit.

"She's well, and the boys." Daniel shook his head. "The baby crawled out of the house and ate something that disagreed with her, Sarah told my Elizabeth. Was sick for a couple of days.

"They're hungry all the time. It's hard to teach children something's poisonous when what they see is beautiful red leaves or fat purple berries. If you're half-starved, you eat; if you're lucky, you live. What do babies know about danger? I worry for them. All of them. With that creek running along the edge of their place, too. Sarah needs someone to help her."

"I'm on my way over there now with the rest of this wood." Matthew untied Lady's reins and climbed into the driver's seat. "My last stop for the day."

Daniel rested his hand on the farmer's boot and shook it gently. "She needs a husband, Sarah. Think about it."

"I have, Daniel. But everyone I know is older, married. You and Elizabeth are closer to her age. Don't you know someone?" Matthew, who had been gazing toward the distant range of blue hills, looked down into his friend's upturned face.

"We should be able to come up with something." Daniel backed away from the wagon and walked alongside it toward the road. "Thanks again for the wood. I've finished the shoes for Tom's older children; should have the third pair next time I see you."

"Why is he so stubborn?" Daniel set his spoon in his bowl. Two hours after dark, the children were asleep and he and his wife were finally eating supper. "He knows Sarah needs help. And he has that big place and all the strength and skill to run it. The woman may not survive a winter without a husband, a father for those children. And our Matthew takes her a sack of flour and a stack of wood."

Elizabeth grinned as though she knew something

he'd overlooked. "You do brighten my day, my dear."

"The man has eyes: He must know she's beautiful." Daniel pushed aimlessly at his stew with the spoon.

"That may be part of the problem." Elizabeth set her empty dish in the basin on the table by the window and sat back down next to him with her cup of tea. "She's so beautiful, and young, that Matthew may not have considered the possibility. May never, on his own. Perhaps you can find some way to put the idea into his head that doesn't require a hammer. And the sooner the better."

A few days later Daniel put the three pairs of children's shoes into a bag with a jar of Elizabeth's berry jam. Ordinarily he would have waited for Matthew's next trip to town, but the nights were getting cold and his neighbors were preparing to harvest their last crops. There was no time to waste.

He walked the road the farmers traveled in their carts, waving greetings to men in their fields. Orchard trees bowed under the weight of apples and pears.

He found Matthew at the workbench in the barn, turning a slender maple post on the lathe. Setting his sack out of the way on a nearby stool, Daniel lifted another post off the stack.

"Balustrade?"

As Matthew untied his tool apron and tossed it onto the table, one string fell off onto the floor. "I don't know." He leaned down to pick up the length of linen tape and laid it next to the apron.

"You've got sixteen . . . eighteen posts here. What do you mean you don't know?"

"I've been making them for something. I'm just not sure what." When Matthew pushed his hair back off his forehead, Daniel noticed a small tear in his sleeve and a button missing from his shirtfront.

"Well, this is a puzzle. But then, you are a puzzling man." He brought the bag to the workbench and set the jam jar to one side before he laid out the small pairs of shoes next to each other.

"Fine workmanship, Daniel. They'll last a good long time. Maybe even long enough to hand down to the younger children, although they grow like weeds, Tom's three. Taller and stronger every time I see them. Take care of themselves. And each other." He seemed distracted. "How is Sarah's little girl?"

"Better now. But she was very sick for a couple of days. Sarah was beside herself."

Matthew picked up the post he'd been working. "I was thinking about a little enclosure, for the child, so she could be out of doors in the good weather and kept out of harm at the same time."

"A baby coop." Daniel grinned.

"Something like that. How is Sarah? Have you seen her recently?"

"Yesterday. She looked the way she always does now, tired and careworn. The other women help as much as they're able, with their own families to care for."

Daniel lifted the stick out of the farmer's hands and

set it gently on the bench. Then he grabbed Matthew's shoulders as though he might shake something into him—sense, or guilt even. "We fear for her: She can't support her family here, on her own, and she has no people to go to, since her father died."

Matthew twisted out of Daniel's grip and turned away, head bowed. "God knows, I'm painfully aware of her situation. If I weren't old enough to be her father, homely as an ox, and more than half used up, I'd marry her myself. If she'd have me . . . which she wouldn't."

"Have you ever asked her?"

" She can hardly abide my presence, Daniel, much less my company. Poor old dog that I am."

Matthew finished laying the maple posts in an evenly-spaced row on the workbench. They looked like a thin picket fence. "Can't figure out how to connect them without making it rigid. Think it would be better if she could roll it up, even, and stow it somewhere when it rains. Sarah, I mean."

Side by side they gazed at the sticks and considered solutions.

Daniel broke the silence. "What makes you think she dislikes you? I'm sure she cares for you, as much as we do. We all do. What's gotten into you?"

Matthew toyed with the sticks, moving them closer together, then farther apart. "I took her some wood, the day I brought yours. Stacked it along the wall where she wanted it. Thought I'd done exactly as she asked, so that it would stay dry. And she got . . . well, angry, I think, is the only way to say it."

"Angry? What happened?"

"Nothing out of the ordinary. I took her a bag of flour, apples, clothes that Tom's children have outgrown. Stacked the wood. Just about to leave and suddenly she was in tears. I can't imagine . . ."

But Daniel had begun to get the drift. "What did she say, Matthew?"

"Say?"

"Did she thank you for the stack of wood?"

"Yes. And for the flour and apples."

"And the clothes for the children?"

"Yes. There was one shirt she liked especially, with a bit of embroidery on the pocket. And a dress her baby will be able to wear soon enough." His smile, recalling their chat, faded as abruptly as Sarah's happiness had.

"What else?" Daniel remembered his wife's good-humored plea for gentleness.

Matthew's forehead was as furrowed as a spring field. "What else?"

"I'm wondering what Sarah's given you."

Matthew was startled to anger. "You know as well as I do, the woman has almost nothing. She's struggling to keep her family going with the little help we can give her. She doesn't need even more demands on her thin resources." His rising voice agitated the swallows in the rafters and hung in the air just long enough

47

for the sense of Daniel's question to catch up with him.

"A jar of maple syrup," he mumbled, turning to look out the door. "Part of a jar."

"How would you feel if you knew that everyone thought you were so poor they wouldn't even let you contribute what you were able to offer them?"

"Even worse," Matthew whispered.

"I've got to get home. Take care, my friend. Be as generous with your needs as you are with your gifts." Daniel patted Matthew's shoulder and walked through the barn door into the golden light of late afternoon.

"Good night," Matthew called after him. He picked up a small shoe and smoothed the soft leather with his fingers. "Thank you."

Two days later, Matthew tapped on Sarah Carpenter's open door with a blanket-wrapped bundle under his arm. She turned from the stove to greet him.

"Matthew, what a surprise! I didn't hear your horse. Please come in. Will you have some water?"

"It's such a clear, cool day I decided to walk." He set his parcel on the table and sat on the small, wobbly chair. "A drink of water would be a pleasure."

He took the cup from her hand. "Thank you."

Through the open door he could see the boys combing the roadside ditch for kindling twigs. He turned to look at the baby, lying on the bed, playing with her toes.

"How is she?"

"Much better, thank you. We had a worrisome day or two, but she seems to have recovered well." Sarah was standing so close to his shoulder that he could feel her warmth through his shirt sleeve.

"I have a favor to ask. Although I know how busy you are with the children, a household to run."

"What can I do for you?" She laid a hand lightly on his shoulder.

He opened the bundle on the table. "I have shirts, stockings, other things that need mending, and I don't do it myself. Can't see well enough to thread a needle, to tell the truth. Since Hannah died the holes just get bigger. Do you suppose . . ."

"I'd be glad to. With growing boys, I'm always patching and darning. What's this?" She opened a cloth packet on top of the stack of garments.

"Some yarns, scissors, needles of Hannah's that I thought you might need to do the work." He stood and held her hand for a moment. "Thank you for your help." Her blue eyes held him. And the voice in his head that spoke to God as he planted and harvested his crops whispered *Beloved*.

DRAGON'S BLOOD

Can I be said to have put those ideas in the boy's head? Surely it had as much to do with the Old Testament name they gave him as with any Greek myth I read to my students: Gideon, the farmer's son turned warrior, who saved his people from the Midianites by courage and cunning.

Gideon Wright learned the alphabet standing at Matthew's shoulder as he read Bible verses to the family before sleep. The boy pointed to a letter to ask its name and sound. Was so interested in Elijah's ride to Heaven in the chariot of fire that Matthew and Sarah made a point of steering him clear of coals and candles lest he get into some mischief and burn down the barn.

At fourteen, Gideon still attended school after the last crops were in, until the farmers sowed in spring. Matthew plowed, the oxen being too strong and stubborn for the boy to shift. Once the beasts determine to stand or walk their own way, it takes a mighty heave on the reins to direct them elsewhere.

I came here from Boston when my sister returned there to marry Will Foster. We had both attended a school for teachers in that city. And while my sister had been pleased to teach children here to read and write and do such sums as would be helpful in the running of a farm or other business, I grew ever more eager to bring other matters to their attention. I knew most of them would never leave this valley and thought it was good for them to know that the world is larger and more varied than their wildest imaginings.

Most of my pupils had never seen any book but the family Bible. I told them of the great library at Alexandria and its descendants in the cities; of the printing presses where a person can buy a book about a subject that interests him, or a map, of a particular city or the entire world, of the oceans or the heavens.

Matthew told me that he once asked what story he had overheard Gideon telling his sister, and the boy said it was an old Greek tale I had read my students, about Jason and his crew and their search for a fleece of gold. Gideon asked Matthew how any sheep could enter the world or live under the crushing weight of a golden pelt. Although in the story it was the fleece Jason ran after, not the sheep, which had already been killed for its hide, the boy's first concern was for the freakish beast.

Gideon didn't share with his sister or anyone else the story that gripped his imagination hard enough to inspire the inventiveness for which he later became famous. I had modified the tales of Jupiter's amorous exploits to protect my young listeners, ending with his kidnapping of Princess Europa. I hurried through the story of her brother's failed attempt to rescue her, in order to get on to the more important business of the founding of Thebes. The prince's slaying of the dragon and sowing its teeth raised no questions among my students that afternoon.

The power of the myth of Cadmus only came to light in our community the day of Mr. Moon's marriage to Miss Sophie Bell. Since Mr. Moon was our magistrate and his bride was moving here to live, the service and celebration were to be held in his church rather than her family's at Lowell.

As we later learned, Gideon chose what he knew was his father's best field, where the woods had been cleared two generations ago, and each flooding of the creek lays down another layer of rich loam.

On Good Friday, while the family took food to the sick, the boy had returned to the house and taken the red stone necklace from the pocket of his mother's heavy black winter coat. He had cut the old cord with a knife and emptied the beads into the linen scarf, which he carried to the field by the creek.

Imagining how Cadmus must have sown his dragon's teeth, Gideon planted each red stone in a narrow hole ten inches deep, several paces from the last, to accommodate the rising up of a new race of warriors who would come to his call and obey his commands. Two staggered rows of single beads, six or eight feet apart, in unmarked graves.

His troops had not arisen on Easter—as he had hoped, having no idea of the time for gestation of an army from the earth, but only that of a god-made-man—nor had they emerged when he checked the site of his careful experiment again and again, to find a flawless carpet of dense green grass.

Greater dismay rocked the household weeks later, when Sarah discovered that the necklace, her only permanent link to the mother who had died releasing her into the world, was missing.

In such a small community, everyone is invited to each wedding, christening, and funeral, to celebrate our lives together in the church we all attend. On the late June morning of Mr. Moon's marriage, Matthew was standing on the porch with the children in their best clothes when Sarah came to the door and beckoned him inside.

"I can't find my mother's necklace. Have you seen it?" She frowned and reached again into the deep pockets of the heavy black coat, flung on their bed like a shot crow.

"I haven't seen it since you wore it at our own wedding. Might you have put it away someplace else? Or moved it since then?"

"I keep it always in my mother's coat pocket since my father gave it to me. Wrapped in her linen scarf."

"We'll search for it as soon as we get home: It can't have gone far without feet."

Oblivious to the bright day, deaf to the ceremony and happy conversation afterwards, bereft of appetite for cake and tea, Gideon had sneaked away from the people among whom he'd grown up—people who loved and trusted him—to rush back to the field, where the grass was a foot tall. He burrowed like a gopher until dusk and never found even one red bead, one drop of dragon's blood.

Returning home defeated, he'd confessed his crime, a theft so heinous . . . and at the same time an escapade of such imagination . . . that the shock moved Sarah to rare tears.

Matthew scythed that field the next day as if he were cutting a baby's cornsilk hair with scissors. He plowed a wide border, his first furrows parallel to the creek, then a series of short rows perpendicular to those, and uncovered three red beads. The others hid in their earthen wombs so stubbornly that Gideon wondered if he'd buried them upside down, if his army had sprung instead, by some terrible accident, on the other side of the world.

I answered my door one morning a week later to find Sarah on the stoop and invited her into the kitchen, where we sat over cups of tea. She reached into her pocket and set one red bead on the table between us. By now the entire community knew of Gideon's experiment.

"Behold: the soldier!" I picked up the stone to admire its color.

"I don't know what to do with it. Or him. He is such a puzzle, to Matthew and to me. And now doesn't say anything, or play, but only works hard and looks sad. I know he feels bad, and I don't know what to do about it. Matthew has tried to talk with him, but it's almost as though he's deaf."

"Perhaps I can speak to him."

She frowned. "I'm not sure he'll come. He's so ashamed, he doesn't even talk with us right now."

"Then I shall come to him. Tomorrow. Where will he be working?"

"I'll ask him to pick the beans and tomatoes. You'll find him south of the house, near the road."

I interrupted Gideon's weeding the next morning and led him to a shady place by the creek, far enough from the house that none of the other children would intrude on our conversation.

He was subdued, as his mother had said, politely refusing the rolls I had spread with a thick layer of peach jam especially to appeal to a boy's appetite intensified by work.

He drank deeply from the creek and splashed his face. I glanced at his profile, beaded with water, and realized that he was growing into manhood in the lean way of these farmers, the planed cheek and narrow nose, long arms and legs, bony knobs of shoulders like the granite boulders they clear from their fields.

Shortly after his confession to his parents, he had cut his own hair close to the scalp, Sarah told me. The precedents in literature have to do with expiation and slavery. Priesthood. Execution.

We sat in silence long enough for the water to dry on his face.

"Gideon?"

He turned his steady gaze on me then, and I knew that he would soon leave us, lured off the farm by the fates, or driven away when the furies discovered an expansive temperament trapped by the very soil he had hoped would generate comrades in arms. There was no one in this valley for him to lead, nothing to inspire him further. No painter ever caught the cool grey-green of those eyes in a portrait, or conveyed their capacity to assess terrain, conditions, company.

Thirty years later, Gideon Wright came to visit me, on the afternoon they buried his mother. He had aged to drift-wood, dense with experience, lathed of extraneous tissue, speech and gesture. Eyes still the color of sage leaves. We chatted about his family, about his plans to return eventually and farm Matthew's place. But he never did.

He led troops until the generals recognized his greater gift for inspiring and training them. Even now he is growing the new country's first crop of generals at the school in New York.

When the teapot was empty and the plate of cookies reduced to crumbs, he pulled a silver watch out of his vest pocket to check the time. "It's gotten late. I mustn't keep you longer. Oh, but you'll remember these." Smiling, he drew the fob from the opposite pocket, three red stone beads on a silver wire loop threaded through the last link of the watch chain. "My *first soldiers,* Mother called them.

She gave them to me when I received my commission."

Later Gideon gave one drop of the dragon's blood to each of his sons, Jack and Matthew, as they enrolled in the army college at West Point; and the last one to his daughter Mary on the birth of her son.

It was Gideon's Jack who married Kate Shoemaker, who inherited the tool chest that Matthew Wright had made for her grandfather. Kate wrapped Daniel Shoemaker's worn hammers and awls in oiled cloth and lay them at the back of a closet shelf. She stored the family table silver in the cherry wood chest that sat on the sideboard in their dining room in Albany.

WESTWARD MOVEMENT

NEW DREAMS FOR OLD!
NEW LIVES FOR OLD!

Once Missouri was no longer the frontier and St. Louis had become the gateway to the West, families from the crowded cities of the Atlantic seaboard arrived to help build the new town at the trading post on the bluff above the Mississippi River.

The newcomers believed that anyone could be whatever he could dream of becoming. Not only the adventurers heading into the unknown, but the people in St. Louis who provisioned their journeys, left their pasts behind them in order to devote their energies to fulfilling their ambitions and creating new worlds.

Ruth Wright was born in 1930 in St. Louis, the only child of a doctor and the daughter of a local department store owner.

Ruth never met her father's family, military people from New York. But by 1915, her mother's father, Grandpa Newman, had parlayed his horse-and-buggy notions sales into a department store that occupied half a block downtown on Olive Street. His wife, Ruth's grandmother, took to her role as one of the young city's society hostesses. She was delighted when their daughter married a doctor who joined and then inherited his father's successful practice, which allowed Ruth's mother to fulfill social ambitions only slightly less imposing than her parents'.

Ruth was the first woman in her family to attend university. In her junior year, she married Martin Twist, a World War II veteran attending law school on the GI Bill. After graduation, she taught in the local high school while Martin finished his coursework and passed the bar. When Joe was born she stayed home to raise him and run the household.

Ruth inherited the worn cherry wood box, which may have held tools once upon a time and had been in her father's family for generations. Small compartments in the upper drawer held earrings, pins, collar stays and studs Ruth remembered from evenings in her childhood when her parents dressed to attend the opera or theater. Larger sections in the front of the lower drawer held necklaces of amber, jet, and amethyst. Three strands of perfectly matched pearls with a sapphire clasp. At the back of the drawer, among a jumble of derelict brooches and pendants, earrings with bent clips or chipped cloisonné, and a short string of pink coral flowers, lay a solitary red stone bead that might, at first glance, have been mistaken for a marble.

As she grew older, Ruth wanted to learn about her ancestors, but her parents and grandparents were gone. Ruth was the last apple on her mother's family tree. With the help of her son Joe and grandson Henry, she used the genealogical information available in the library and on-line to trace her father's family as far back as the birth of a daughter in early Boston. She even went to visit the church and read the entry carefully penned in a worn, heavy volume in the sacristy:

Sarah Willing . . . born March 8, 1745.

And in the same hand, on the line just below:

Mary Willing . . . died March 8, 1745.

Seeing those notations in rusty black ink on thick pages freckled with years made her family history as real as the toast she'd eaten that morning.

Her further researches revealed Ruth's relationship by blood to Lady Mary Guildford, whose portrait by Hans Holbein hangs downtown in the St. Louis Art Museum.

THE MOONAGATE SHOOTER

LAST OCTOBER, IN A CITY A FEW HOURS
FROM HERE BY SEVERAL DAILY NON-STOP
FLIGHTS, TWO BOYS TRADED KNOWLEDGE AND
SKILLS FOR FRIENDSHIP, UNDERSTANDING . . .
AND A RED MARBLE.

Henry Twist brought his marbles to school every day in a thick green cotton sock, the mate to which had disappeared on a trip to the lake. He tied the cuff in a loose knot to keep the marbles from spilling out. He had a fine collection of agates, steelies and puries. He also had a strong thumb and a deadly aim.

Henry won marbles and traded marbles. He ruled, in that corner of Walker Elementary playground where his classmates crouched in a circle to watch him capture other kids' marbles to add to his growing stash.

In the middle of fall term, Henry's fifth-grade teacher, Ms. Whatley, had called to alert his parents that Henry was what she termed *a slow learner.* Which Henry's mom understood as *in need of tutoring,* and Henry took to mean some kind of *disabled.*

That's when Henry started referring to his teacher as *Ms. What-for* at home, and *Ms. What-a-pain-in-the-butt* at the marble ring, where he'd learned everything he needed to know faster than anyone else, not that Ms. Whatley knew or cared about that.

"Henry, let's go get some ice cream." Joe Twist handed his son the larger of the two Cardinals baseball caps from the hooks by the front door and set the smaller one on the top his own very large, square head.

Only the bridge of Henry's nose stopped the bigger cap's downward slide and kept it from engulfing most of his face. He laughed when his dad grinned, but he sensed that a bribe was in the works. No one, not even Henry's mom, thought of his dad as a clown.

Drastic situations call for drastic measures, said the small voice in Henry's head.

"What say we walk down to A Zillion Improbable Flavors and see what's the weirdest combo they can scoop onto a sugar cone?"

Henry's dad hated Franklin's 57 Flavors. He had said so often enough: He'd prefer to drive to Abilene—wherever that was—for what he called a legitimate, non-emulsified gelato than walk the four blocks from their house for a scoop of caramel snickerdoodle and a scoop of Dangerfield's devil's food (Henry's current favorites) on a waffle cone. Which entire assemblage, as Joe was quick to point out, set him back *two seventy-five per, for godsake!*

Henry knew from experience that the proposal his dad was about to spring on him was going to be just about as repulsive as that double-decker cone was going to be delicious. His dad was a broker: He thought about cost, value, and risk all day long. It was his job. He liked to say, "You gotta size things up, Henry—figure out what you're willing to pay, or give up, in order to get what you think you want."

Not what you want, mind you: What you *think* you want. That was what he said, and Henry knew it was an important difference, even if he didn't quite get it.

Henry figured if his dad was offering two scoops at Franklin's he wanted something Henry wasn't going to like. At all. Was probably going to dislike as much as his dad disliked what he called Franklin's plastic ice cream. Maybe more.

They were three blocks from home, just passing the shoe repair shop, when Henry's dad mentioned school. Math class. English. Ms. Whatley's *concerns*.

Franklin's door had banged shut but the bell was still jingling on its spring when the word *tutor* was finally sitting on the glass in front of Henry, drying its black newborn baby bat wings in the draft from the air conditioning unit.

"I don't need a tutor," Henry said, trying to see past the dark fluttering into the colorful bins in the case.

"Ms. Whatley thinks it would be a good idea for you to get some individual help with a subject or two, just until you've caught up with your classes."

Henry barely heard the man he'd always thought of as Mr. Franklin ask what they'd like.

"I don't think we're quite ready to order yet," Joe said. "Henry, know what you want?"

"I don't want a tutor." He addressed his preference as quietly as possible to the untouched bin of acid green stuff labeled Edible Hulk.

Joe peered into the case. "How about a scoop of Snickerdoodle and a scoop of Devil's Food . . . on a sugar cone? What do you say?"

Henry's face felt as hot as a stove. He wanted to press his forehead against the cold glass. More than that, he wanted, urgently, not to be where he was. Not to be involved in this . . . *skit*, or whatever . . . with his father, who was usually a pretty good guy.

To keep the water from actually running out of his eyes, Henry leaned the side of his face against the glass and watched the creature—more a moth than a bat, really, seen this close—fan its wings slowly, sending him a message no one else could read. *Your eyes only.*

"I guess we're still thinking, thanks. Henry?" His dad's voice had an edge to it. "We'd better place an order pretty quick, so Mr. . . ."

"Benjamin," the man said, almost too quietly for Henry to hear over the rackety hum of the air conditioner.

". . . Mr. Benjamin can get on with things. He's a busy man. Help us out here, Henry."

Time is money, said the voice in Henry's head.

"A fool and his money," Henry replied, to something that had been said . . . or not quite said. He wasn't sure. Just like he wasn't sure where that fool had come from at just that moment.

". . . are soon parted," said Mr. Benjamin, and he winked at Henry. "Clever boy you got there," he said to Henry's dad. "Puts two and two together, that one. So many of them come in here, know from nothing. You know what I'm saying? But you got a smart one there. Not mouthing off like a lot of them. You wouldn't believe some of the things I hear. Take my word for it. No manners. All the time throwing their weight around like they know something.

"So what'll you have, Henry?" Mr. Benjamin nudged a couple of the bins. "I got some new this afternoon: Meadowlark Lemon. New Orleans Bluesberry. Saw you looking at that Edible Hulk, which I haven't even tasted. We oughta test drive that one, see what you think."

He shaved a bit of strange green ice cream onto two tiny plastic spoons and offered them to Henry and his dad, then scooped out a bit for himself and licked it off his own little spoon. Mr. Benjamin *mmmmmm*'d like a hive of bees.

"It's good! You never know. The guy tells me it's a winner in Chicago, someplace, but that doesn't mean folks here will go for it. What do you think, you two?"

Henry's dad hummed and nodded, without actually saying anything, which was about as close as he ever came to lying.

Henry said, "I'd like a scoop of that on a sugar cone, please. And a scoop of Chocomania."

"Wow! Not many of my customers would take on a combination like that." Mr. Benjamin handed Henry a mountainous brown and green cone that looked as though it must live above the timber line somewhere really cold. The Yukon, maybe.

"Now, what about you?" Mr. Benjamin turned to Henry's dad, who was holding out a five-dollar bill.

"We just finished dinner; I'm too full to even think about dessert, Mr. Benjamin, but thanks anyway."

Mr. Benjamin waved away the bill. "On the house, for my friend here."

Walking home, Henry focused his attention on staying ahead of the drips.

"How's that cone, Henry? Good flavors?"

Henry waved to Mr. Bledsoe, who was locking the door of his shoe repair shop. "Hey, Mr. Bledsoe!"

"Hey, Henry!" Mr. Bledsoe called. "How are things going?"

"Henry, we need to talk . . ." Joe said.

"Everything's fine," Henry shouted. "How are you?"

"Henry!" Joe called after him, as Henry trotted to the newsstand in front of the drugstore to read the headlines and take the last bite of Chocomania. "Henry, we need to talk about school."

Henry couldn't think of one thing he needed to talk

about less. He jogged the last block, up the front path, and into the house, trailing green drops of Edible Hulk and leaving the front door open behind him.

"Henry!" his mother called as he took the stairs two at a time. He was in his bedroom by the time Joe entered the house and shut the front door a little harder than was absolutely necessary.

"Joe?" Henry's mom called after him as he followed Henry up the stairs. "What's going on, you two?" She came out of the kitchen, wiping her hands on a dishtowel. "Joe! Henry!"

"Henry, we have to talk about this. Now." Joe knocked on Henry's bedroom door.

Henry opened the door a narrow crack and looked up at his dad. "I don't want a tutor," he said. "There's nothing *wrong* with me."

"Nobody says there is, Henry." His mom was standing at the top of the stairs now, behind his dad and off to one side. "The point is, when you fall behind in your school-work, it can be hard to catch up without help. In fact, what usually happens is that someone falls even farther behind, bit by bit."

"Like what we were saying about debt and interest payments," his dad added. "Remember?"

"Compounded?" Henry eased the door open a bit.

"That's right. And getting behind in your classes can work that way too. Ms. Whatley said that another student who's good at English and math might be able to help you for a while, catch up with assignments where you're behind, and maybe even get a little ahead so that you wouldn't have to work quite so hard afterwards."

It all sounded so reasonable, the way they were putting it, that Henry was having a hard time keeping a grip on his annoyance, but the little gnawing sound at the back of his mind was getting louder as they stood outside his bedroom door, with his dad leaning against the bannister, pulling at his earlobe, a sure sign that he was planning something—what he called *strategizing*.

"Roger Lim," Henry's mother said. "Ms. Whatley told us maybe Roger Lim could help you with your schoolwork."

"Roger Lim!" Henry couldn't believe his ears. "Roger Lim is a dork. He doesn't know how to shoot marbles or play soccer or softball. He wears shiny black shoes and rides a bike that should be in a museum. Roger Lim: You've got to be joking! You're joking, right?" Henry looked at his mother, who turned and walked back down the stairs; then at his father, who had stopped pulling at his earlobe and stared at him.

"Roger Lim lives with his grandmother and rides the bike that used to belong to his grandfather, who ran the drugstore on Alder Street until he died last year," Joe said quietly. "Roger's grandmother is trying to keep the business going and save enough money to send him to college when the time comes.

"He helps her every day after school and works hard

on his studies so that he can go to college someday. If he hasn't developed any skill at marbles, it could be because he doesn't have much time to play games."

Henry felt like a jerk. At the same time, he felt jerked around: Roger Lim's family's problems weren't his problems, for Pete's sake! He didn't know if he was sad or pissed off . . . or both at once. He did know that he'd better not say what he was thinking—that Roger Lim's grandma's bad style sense didn't qualify Roger to tutor Henry in math and English.

"You might have something to offer him too."

"Like what?"

"You're really good at marbles. You've got friends. You're a nice guy. Most of the time, anyway." His dad reached over, pulled off the cap, and rumpled Henry's hair. "Think about it: Maybe you guys could arrange a trade of some sort."

At 7:15 the next morning, Henry's dad paid a visit to the house where he'd grown up.

"Joe? Where are you going?" Ruth asked as her son, dressed for the office, opened the back kitchen door and trotted past her and up the hall stairs.

"Attic, Ma. Just want to check something. Won't be a minute," Joe called back over his shoulder. "Oh! Morning, Ma!" He climbed the narrow wooden stairs at the far end of the second floor and pushed open the trap door above his head until it rested against the attic wall.

The room under the eaves reminded him of a wooden boat, a small ark, come to rest keel-up on top of his mother's house. The ceiling seemed a lot lower than it had when he was a kid and could stand almost anywhere, with room to spare. October sunlight yellowed the roller shade on the small sash window. The cool, still air smelled faintly of soap, mothballs, and the dust of years.

Joe moved aside the stack of faded department store dress boxes containing Christmas ornaments to find the wood-ribbed trunk that in his childhood had held out-of-season clothes and blankets. The lid was locked. The big key hung on a cup hook screwed into a dormer beam right above it.

Typical, Joe thought, *lock the trunk and leave the key where anyone with half a brain can find it.* His parents had grown up in a world where nobody locked their doors; sometime during his own youth they'd started locking the front door, but his mother still left the back door open, for her own convenience, and so that a neighbor in need could help herself to sugar or the phone.

The key turned stiffly in the lock, and Joe opened the lid to find what he was looking for in a corner of the shallow tray right on top: A soft chamois pouch with something lumpy and heavy inside.

"Are you finding what you're after?" his mother called from the foot of the attic stairs.

"Yes, Ma. They're right where I remembered." He closed and locked the trunk and hung the key back on

70

its hook, then climbed back down the stairs, closing the trapdoor over his head as he descended.

"What's that?" She took the bag from Joe's extended hand and tugged it open to peer inside. "Marbles! I don't remember these. Where were they?"

"In the trunk," Joe said. "They were mine, in school, and I think Henry's old enough now, he might like to have them."

Henry poured the marbles out of the bag onto his dark blue bedspread. There were a few really nice agates, a few cat's eyes, some large and small puries, and odds and ends. He'd never seen anything like the three big grey ones that felt like rocks, or the red one with a tiny hole through it. When he looked up, his dad was still standing in the doorway.

"What are these?" He lifted a grey marble between his thumb and index finger to feel its weight and look at the grainy surface, which was smooth but unpolished.

"Granite," Joe said. "They used to be fairly common, but you don't see them very often anymore. Glass marbles have pretty much taken over."

"I've never seen one like this. You mean they're made out of rocks?"

"Yup. They're cut out of granite and then shaped and smoothed."

"But I could shoot them, just like this?"

"That's right." His dad sat down gently on the foot of

the bed and the red marble rolled slowly toward his thigh. He picked it up and held it to the light from Henry's desk lamp. "And this one was my lucky shooter. Feel how smooth that is?"

"What's the hole for?" Henry held the red stone marble up to the light at just the right angle to find a pinprick of light coming through.

"Well, it may actually be a bead. But as long as I can remember it was in with my marbles. And it just seemed to roll better than any of the others. Won some fine agates and puries with it."

"I didn't know you played marbles." Henry couldn't imagine what his father must have been like as a fifth-grader. Tried to picture his six-foot-two-inch frame folded up like a grasshopper at the edge of the circle, red marble in the curl of his index finger, thumb cocked behind, ready to shoot.

"I played a lot. But I didn't have much control. Wasn't nearly as good as you are."

"Really?"

"Yeah. I've watched you, and you're really good, Henry. There are a couple of things you can do when you're that good at something: You can just do it and get better and better and take pride in your abilities. But sometimes you can teach someone who isn't so good, help him shine a little too."

Henry nodded slowly; he knew they were talking about Roger Lim. He'd heard his father say it on the phone in his home office: *Time to fish or cut bait.* And here it was.

"I don't know what to do." Henry couldn't imagine walking up to Roger Lim and asking for help with his schoolwork.

"Don't complicate things, Henry. It doesn't have to be a big deal," his dad said.

Yeah, right. Henry's dad had never had to ask anyone for help. He was the head of an entire department. He assigned projects and told people what to do and how to do it. As far as Henry knew, the only person his dad didn't tell what to do was Henry's mom.

Mrs. Lim rinsed a teacup in the sink in the back room of the pharmacy, her back to the boy crouching over a pair of shoes with a stained rag in his hand.

"If you want to learn how to play this game, you must watch them play it. See who is the best player and watch how he does it. Ask him to show you. Watch very carefully to see what is different about the way he plays, what makes him better than the others. And then do what he does. And then . . ."

"Practice, practice, *practice.* Yes, Grandma, I know." Roger Lim set his newly polished shoes on a square of newspaper by the door to the alley. He had learned how to polish shoes from his grandfather; he could see his face reflected in the black leather surface.

Roger couldn't imagine asking Henry Twist for the

secrets of his success at the marble ring. Even if Henry would talk to him, Roger felt it was . . . highly unlikely that he could imitate Henry's approach, his style. While he couldn't argue with his grandmother, Roger knew he wouldn't approach Henry. Not even if his grandmother insisted, although her word was law in their household.

Once she had told him, "Do not come home until you have taken care of this matter." And he had knocked on giant Mrs. Allen's door and apologized for breaking her bedroom window with an erratically thrown baseball.

Roger's grandmother's quiet severity was even scarier than the prospect of Mrs. Allen's anger, which, as it turned out, was non-existent. She thanked Roger for his apology and smiled when she turned down his offer to pay to have the glass replaced.

At some point, he knew, his small white-haired grandmother would deliver a similar ultimatum about the playground. Until then, Roger would lean against the fence and watch the game—see if he couldn't figure it out for himself, without having to ask. But if he couldn't throw a baseball more or less where he wanted it to go, what hope was there that he could ever shoot a small marble straight at another marble to hit it and capture it?

"Roger." His grandmother's voice broke into his thoughts.

"Yes, Grandma?"

"Do not delay. I will not forget about this."

Roger knew better than to groan aloud.

Henry's mother visited Dr. Lim's Pharmacy the following Monday to buy an unnecessary tube of toothpaste and bar of hand soap.

"Good afternoon, Mrs. Lim. How are you?"

"Very well, thank you. And you, and your family?" The usual this and that: weather, Mrs. Lim's business, Mr. Twist's business, the approach of winter. The difficulties of raising bright, stubborn boys.

"Perhaps it is easier with a man in the house." Mrs. Lim shook her head. "Sometimes I think if his grandfather were still here . . ."

"I'm not sure this is a matter for men to deal with," Henry's mother confided. "Henry's father doesn't know what to do right now. He was an eleven-year-old boy himself at one time: Maybe that confuses the issue."

Mrs. Lim's thoughtful gaze slowly turned into a smile. "I was just making a cup of tea. Would you like one?" She opened the gate in the pharmacy counter and Henry's mother followed her into the small workroom in back; every square foot of wall space was lined with narrow shelves crowded with jars and boxes of pills. Mrs. Lim introduced the man who was filling prescriptions as her younger son, Roger's uncle Robert.

Robert Lim looked up and smiled briefly before scraping the pills on the small glass table in front of him into a white envelope and sealing it with a prescription label. Then he pushed back his stool and turned toward them, just as Mrs. Lim gestured toward two chairs in the corner,

75

where an electric kettle was steaming quietly on top of a small bookcase filled with pharmacology reference books and a fat red English dictionary.

"We are just going to have a cup of tea, Robert. Don't let us disturb you."

Robert turned back to his stack of prescription slips. Henry's mother was briefly aware of the quiet rattle, snick and slide as he counted pills into plastic containers.

Mrs. Lim handed her guest a blue and white cup of fragrant amber tea and then poured one for herself. "It is so hard to know how to help sometimes, isn't it?" She sipped her tea and set the cup on the counter. "Roger would like to get to know other children his own age, but he is not sure how."

Mrs. Twist took another sip of her tea and set her cup down next to Mrs. Lim's. She folded her hands in her lap. "Henry has attended Walker Elementary since kindergarten; making friends has always been easy for him. But schoolwork's another matter. He's smart enough to do well, but for some reason he's having a hard time this year. With math and English. His father and I aren't sure what to do about it. He seems reluctant—Henry, that is—to ask his classmates for help."

"It is so difficult. What makes these boys think they have to figure everything out themselves? My grandson: He can stand by the fence and watch the boys play marbles until he is as old as Robert there. If he does not learn from one of the others, he will never feel that he is good enough to play with them."

As she sipped her tea, Henry's mother was again aware of the quiet rattle of pills sliding into little plastic jars at the other end of the counter. "I don't know how to encourage Henry to ask for help."

Mrs. Lim set down her cup and rested her hand lightly on her visitor's wrist. "Roger is a thoughtful boy. If he knows someone is having a difficult time but doesn't know how to ask, maybe he can figure out some other way to offer help." She watched her guest put her mind to work on the possibilities.

Henry wondered just how Roger Lim was having a problem diagramming sentences for English. He was happy to work with him, but Roger seemed to know more about parts of speech than Henry did himself. They sat side by side at a table in the cafeteria that was used as a study hall the last two periods of the day and after school.

"'*Seeing is believing*' is two participles," Roger said. "I think."

Henry had heard the word *participle* before, just as he had heard *preposition* and *superlative,* but they didn't make sense. Ms. Whatley's explanations flew right past him, too fast to understand or remember. And he was afraid to ask questions: He couldn't ask about everything she'd told them about since the very basic stuff right at the beginning, *nouns* and *verbs;* he'd gotten lost at *direct objects* and been wandering around in a thicket of grammar ever since.

"So, *seeing* is a verb that's been made into a noun, and

so is *believing.* Since the verb in the sentence is *to be,* it's maybe like a little equation: *a* equals *b.* Right? I think I'm starting to get it." Roger nodded and glanced at Henry, who was watching him draw a line with the ruler and label the parts of speech.

"I think you understand this stuff better than I do, Roger. I'll probably learn a lot more from working on English assignments together than you will." Henry wasn't exactly sure how this arrangement had come about. Someone . . . his mom? . . . had said that Roger was having a tough time at his new school. It was pretty obvious to Henry that Roger didn't have any problems with English. Or math either.

"It's helpful for me to study with another student," Roger said. "I learn more that way. It's good to know different ways to look at the same problem. Don't you think so? At my old school, we always studied in pairs and groups. It was more fun." Roger's eyes rested on Henry's face for the briefest moment. "We are already on number four. We can be done when we leave here. We will know how to work these problems, not have to do them at home tonight. I think that's good."

Henry nodded. The prospect of getting home with his assignments finished—done right, for a change—was a relief.

By 3:45 they'd finished the English assignment and done six of the math problems. Henry felt he understood the story questions well enough to do the last four on his own. He and Roger zipped their books and papers into their backpacks and walked diagonally across the playground toward the opening in the far corner of the fence. There was no one on the swings or the jungle gym; no one smacking the worn yellow tetherball on its rope. There was no one at the marble ring near the gate.

"Want to play marbles?" Henry eased his pack off his shoulders as they walked and unfastened the side pocket to pull out the green sock full of marbles.

"I don't know how," Roger said. "I mean, I watch, but I've never played. I don't have any marbles."

"Here," Henry said, and emptied the sock on the dirt next to the ring. "You can use some of mine for now. Pick a marble for your shooter."

Roger chose one of the heavy granite marbles, because it looked old and ugly and he figured since there were three of them, they couldn't all be Henry's favorite. Rolling it between his thumb and fingers he noticed the pocked surface.

"Not that one," Henry said, taking the grey marble out of Roger's hand. "That's too heavy to start with, and may not roll very smoothly, on dirt, until you've played for a while. Pick another one."

Roger picked up the red stone marble with the tiny hole through it. "This one," he said, smiling at Henry. "Red is the color for good luck."

"Really?" Henry said. "That was my dad's lucky marble. I've never used it because I always use my blue shooter. And I didn't know if the hole would make any difference. But you can try it; if it doesn't roll right you can use another one."

Roger's aim was lousy, but he focused so hard that Henry thought he might bore holes through the other marbles too. That afternoon, Roger learned how to shoot and the few things about strategy that Henry could describe. Henry's skills were ingrained through long use and his approach was what his dad would have called instinctive: He sized things up and took his best shot confidently. He was used to winning.

Roger borrowed two cat's eyes and a green purie to practice at home. He dedicated twenty minutes every afternoon to shooting marbles on the smooth dirt under the lemon tree behind his grandmother's house.

"Please come to dinner right now." His grandmother looked at Roger, curled like a shrimp in concentration. "I don't want to have to call you one more time."

"Yes, Grandma." Roger scooped up the marbles and dropped them into his pocket. He had gotten the feel of it now, and could tell a good shot from an inferior one. But he was a long way from knowing how to make his shooter go and stop where he wanted it to every time.

Henry didn't know if his math and English skills were improving—it wasn't like marbles, where you could see the results right away—but he enjoyed studying with Roger, and shooting a few rounds with him on the way out of the playground every afternoon.

"Go ahead, Roger," Henry said, plucking the red marble out of the ring.

"Are you sure?" Crouching beside him, Roger frowned at his friend.

"It's your lucky shooter. You won it, fair and square." Henry dropped it into Roger's hand.

When Roger closed the cool stone in his fist and shut his eyes, he could see the girl again, as he had seen her before, a slim, dark girl in baggy striped pants and a dark blue tunic. Around her neck was an entire necklace made of beads the same color as the marble in his hand.

"Ready to go, Grandma?" Roger Lim smiled down at the tiny woman who had raised him. At eighty-five, she was returning to China to visit family members she hadn't seen in more than sixty years. Her brother still lived in the town where they had been born and spent their childhood, a place every bit as exotic to Roger as it would have been to his best friend, Henry Twist, whose ancestors had still been painting their faces blue when merchants of the old dynasties traded silks and stones, spices and livestock along the caravan routes from Huangzhou to Tashkent and Samarkand.

Roger's grandmother opened her suitcase for a final look and pointed to the worn red sewing basket tucked into one corner. The jade ring in the center of the lid could be used as a handle; several beads sewn onto the top were purely decorative.

"There it is." She smiled, and Roger saw the red bead, bigger than the rest, tied in place with a blue silk thread. "Your lucky marble."

"For your safe journey, Grandma." He smoothed the worn red stone with his thumb. *Take it back to where you were both born,* he thought, *back to the start of all the time we can imagine.*

. . . A STORY SO OLD, OR SO NEW,
NOBODY KNOWS WHERE IT BEGINS . . .

A farmer tends his terraced field on the slope of an ancient mountain that thrusts into the clouds like the reaching, broken arm of a tumbled stone god. Despite the rain, it's warm enough that he wears only his oldest pants, rolled up to his knees, and an old straw hat to keep sweat out of his eyes. His toes squelch in mud; his arms, legs and hands, and the cloth bag tied around his neck are glazed with it. He reaches into the sack for another seedling, shoves his staff into the earth, and pushes the infant plant into the hole quickly, before the mud can heal itself.

Already this morning he has planted eight bags of thirty-two seedlings apiece. When he empties the one around his neck, and two more after that, he'll sit on the boulder that marks the corner of his field long enough to drink a cup of tea and let the rain wash this coat of mud off him. For what? So he can start a new one. Ha!

He takes the next seedling from the sack and drives the stick into the mud, where it tocks against something hard. He leans down to scoop up the rock and throw it out of his way. But the stone is round and smooth, unlike others in these fields, and as he holds it up to look more closely, he notices the blood red color, the small round hole drilled through the center. He shouts to his wife, who comes to look and puzzle over it: What is it? Where did it come from? Why is it here? What should we do with it?

Neither of them has dropped such a stone in the field, or seen one like it before. Six holes farther along the row, the farmer finds a second red stone, just like the first. And in the course of the day, twenty-six more, which he drops into the bottom of the bag of seedlings as he works.

That evening, he pours them into a brown pottery bowl full of water. Unsure of their origin, he leaves the bowl on the ground outside the door of the house so that no one can accuse him of theft. Pondering, he squats beside the bowl and runs a hand through the stones to listen to their quiet conversation.

His mother comes to call him in to dinner and watches him rattle the stones as he gazes into the darkness beyond their gate. "What are they? Why are they in your field? This cannot be good: It makes me afraid for you."

"Don't worry." He looks up at her over his shoulder. "They're the color of good fortune, a gift from the gods. We'll let them rest here one day for each stone. If no one claims them in that time, you can string them together, and I'll take them to the next market."

AND THAT IS HOW THE RED STONES
MAKE THEIR WAY TO HUANGZHOU
TO BEGIN THEIR LONG JOURNEY WEST.

HEARTFELT THANKS TO

Milly Glenn and Katie Mills, for instilling in me a profound sense of the ridiculous; and to Russ Mills and John O'Mahony for keeping it alive and in tune.

Brother Bill and sister Penny and their wonderful mates and kids. And to our dad, who would have been pleased to see this day.

A galaxy of extraordinary friends and other family members too numerous to name here.

Hilary Abramson, Peg Bracken, George Keithley, Rebecca Radner, and other writing friends for hours of great chat about stuff nobody else knows or cares about.

John Laursen, Janet Livesay, and Jon Rabinowitz for their generous advice about printing and publishing. And to every librarian and independent bookseller I've ever had the pleasure to know.

Bill Halewood, Alice Wipf, and other teachers who fostered my love of literature and helped refine my critical thinking and writing skills.

King Lau, Cullen Philippson, and the One-to-One team at the Mac Store for technical instruction, setup and backup expertise, as I flail in the margins of these ever-shifting technologies.

And my amazing Tribe—you know who you are—for sharing your stories, strength, hope, and so much laughter.